SpongeBob and the Princess

by David Lewman

illustrated by Clint Bond

SIMON SPOTLIGHT/NICKELODEON

New York   London   Toronto   Sydney

Based on the TV series *SpongeBob SquarePants*® created by Stephen Hillenburg as seen on Nickelodeon®

SIMON SPOTLIGHT
An imprint of Simon & Schuster Children's Publishing Division
1230 Avenue of the Americas, New York, New York 10020
Manufactured in the United States of America
First Edition 10 9 8 7 6 5 4 3 2 1
ISBN 0-689-86581-3

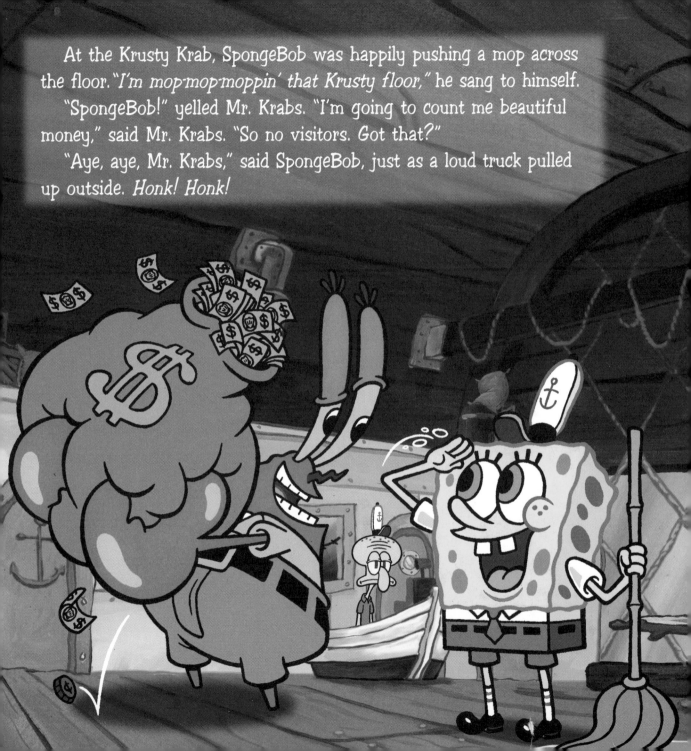

At the Krusty Krab, SpongeBob was happily pushing a mop across the floor. *"I'm mop-mop-moppin' that Krusty floor,"* he sang to himself.

"SpongeBob!" yelled Mr. Krabs. "I'm going to count me beautiful money," said Mr. Krabs. "So no visitors. Got that?"

"Aye, aye, Mr. Krabs," said SpongeBob, just as a loud truck pulled up outside. *Honk! Honk!*

"Welcome to the outside of the Krusty Krab. May I help you?" SpongeBob shouted to the driver, trying to make himself heard over the noise of the truck.

"Where's Mr. Krabs?" the driver asked.

"Counting his money, so he's not to be disturbed," answered SpongeBob. "Maybe I can help you."

"What?" yelled the driver.

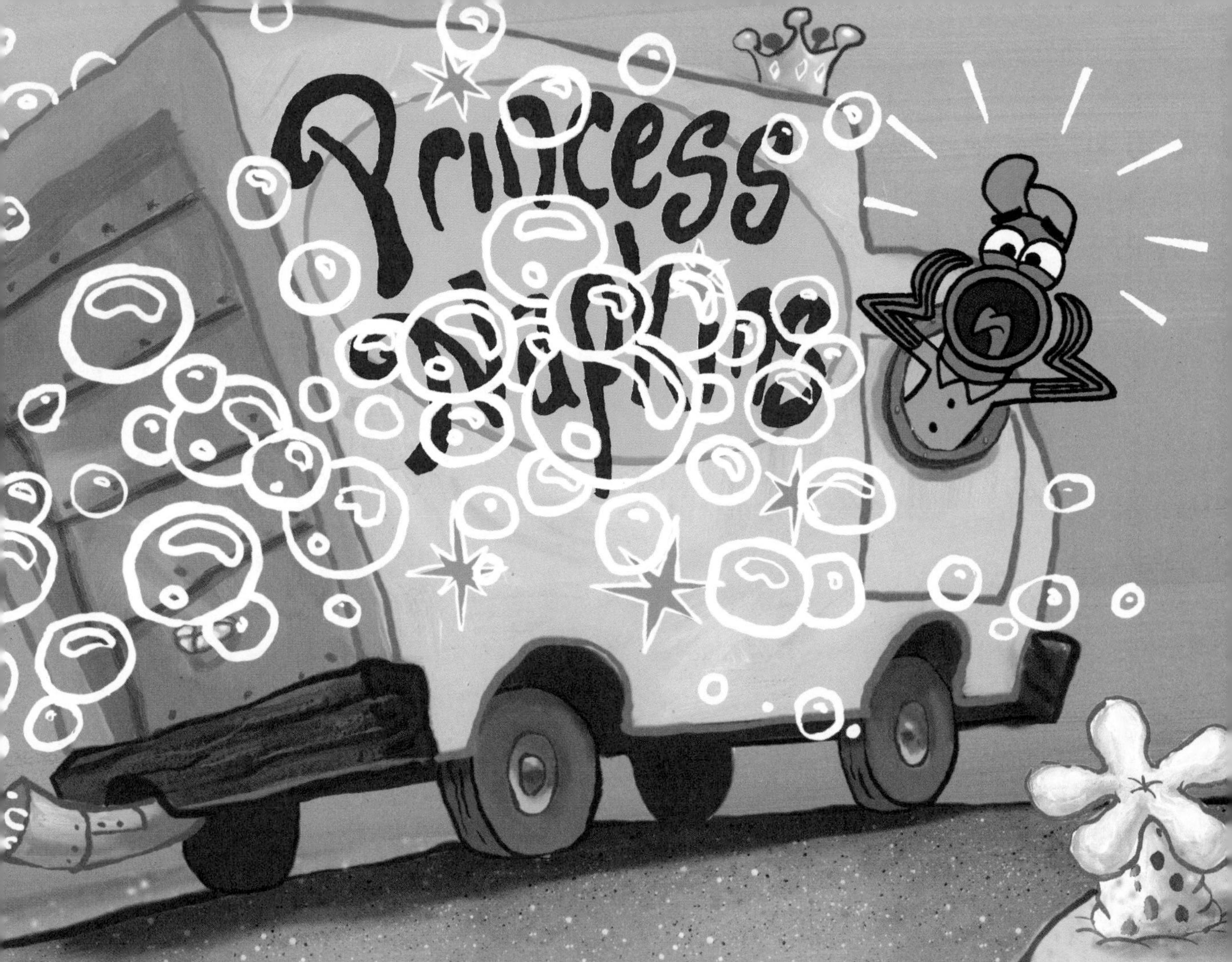
Princess

SpongeBob cupped his hands to his mouth. "Maybe I can help you!"

"Tell Mr. Krabs that Princess Napkins will be here tomorrow," said the driver.

"What?" yelled SpongeBob.

"Princess delivery will be here tomorrow!" the driver shouted back.

"Got it!" said SpongeBob, giving a big thumbs-up. The driver drove off. "Hoppin' clams," said SpongeBob. "Wait till Squidward hears this!"

SpongeBob burst into the Krusty Krab. "Guess what,
Squidward! A princess'll be here tomorrow!"

Squidward didn't look up. "What princess would be caught dead in this dump?"
he asked gloomily. But then he brightened. "Unless it's . . . Princess Neptuna!
It doesn't seem likely, but for once, SpongeBob, I believe you! I *love* royalty!
They're so . . . *royal!*"

SpongeBob grinned. "I can't wait to tell Patrick and Sandy and Mrs. Puff and–"

Squidward shook his head. "No, no, don't tell anyone. Royal people love their privacy." Squidward figured he had a much better chance of getting Princess Neptuna's autograph if no one else was around.

"Really?" said SpongeBob, puzzled. "I thought princesses *loved* crowds."

Squidward sniffed. "You commoner. You know nothing about royalty."

SpongeBob thought hard. "Well, I *have* to tell Mr. Krabs."

"No!" yelled Squidward. "He'll ruin everything."

"But, Squidward," said SpongeBob, "it's my duty as a Krusty Krab employee!"

Squidward put his arm around SpongeBob. "Listen, SpongeBob," he said, "would you like me to teach you how to behave around royalty?"

SpongeBob's eyes grew big. "You'd teach me, Squidward?"

"Of course," said Squidward, smiling.

"Tonight?" asked SpongeBob, his eyes growing even bigger.

"Um, okay," said Squidward.

"At your house?" SpongeBob's eyes were huge. "With snacks?"

Squidward swallowed hard. "Sure, SpongeBob. I'm . . . inviting you . . . to my house . . . for royalty lessons and . . . snacks."

"HOORAY!" SpongeBob shouted. "I'll be there! And tomorrow the princess will be here!"

In his office Mr. Krabs heard SpongeBob shouting. "Better see what me employees are up to," he said, hurrying over to a picture on the wall. He lifted it and peered through a peephole just in time to hear SpongeBob say, "Tomorrow the princess will be here!"

"Princess?" whispered Mr. Krabs. "Princesses are rich! And people love to see 'em. People who could be MY PAYING CUSTOMERS! All I have to do is let everybody know a princess is coming to the Krusty Krab tomorrow! Hmm . . ."

That night Squidward tried to teach SpongeBob how to act properly around a princess. "No, no, SpongeBob," he scolded. "Never giggle when you bow to Princess Neptuna."

"But, Squidward," said SpongeBob. "I can't help it. Patrick looks kinda funny."

Patrick adjusted his crown. "Gee, thanks a lot, SpongeBob," he said. "I think I look beautiful."

Meanwhile Mr. Krabs was busy putting up signs all over Bikini Bottom announcing Princess Neptuna's arrival at the Krusty Krab. He chuckled to himself. "This ought to bring in the customers," he said. "*And their money!*"

As SpongeBob approached the Krusty Krab the next morning, he saw almost all of Bikini Bottom waiting outside. "Gee," he said, "there sure are a lot of people hungry for delicious Krabby Patties today."

Just then Squidward showed up. "Oh, no!" he cried. "They must all be here to see Princess Neptuna!"

He angrily turned to SpongeBob. "You blabbed to everyone about the princess!"

"No, Squidward," answered SpongeBob. "I was over at your house, remember?"

Squidward scrunched up his face in confusion. "Then how did they all find out?"

"RIGHT THIS WAY!" barked Mr. Krabs. "THIS WAY TO SEE THE PRINCESS! CUSTOMERS WITH MONEY ONLY!"

The truck from the day before pulled up. An eager SpongeBob ran over, "When will the princess be here?" he whispered.

The driver scratched his head and gave SpongeBob a blank look.

"Yesterday you told me to tell Mr. Krabs, 'A princess will be here tomorrow,'" explained SpongeBob.

The driver stared at SpongeBob and then started laughing. "I said, 'The Princess delivery will be here tomorrow.' Y'know, *Princess Napkins.*"

SpongeBob's mouth dropped open. "You mean Princess Neptuna isn't coming?"

"Nope," the driver replied, unloading several boxes onto the ground. "But here are your napkins. See ya!"

SpongeBob stared at the boxes. "What good are napkins when I promised everyone a princess?" he thought aloud.

SpongeBob spotted Patrick walking by. "Patrick!" he said. "Am I glad to see you! I need you to dress up as the princess again to fool that big crowd of customers!"

Patrick shook his head. "No way, SpongeBob. Last night you said I looked funny."

"Yeah, but . . . but," said SpongeBob, sputtering.

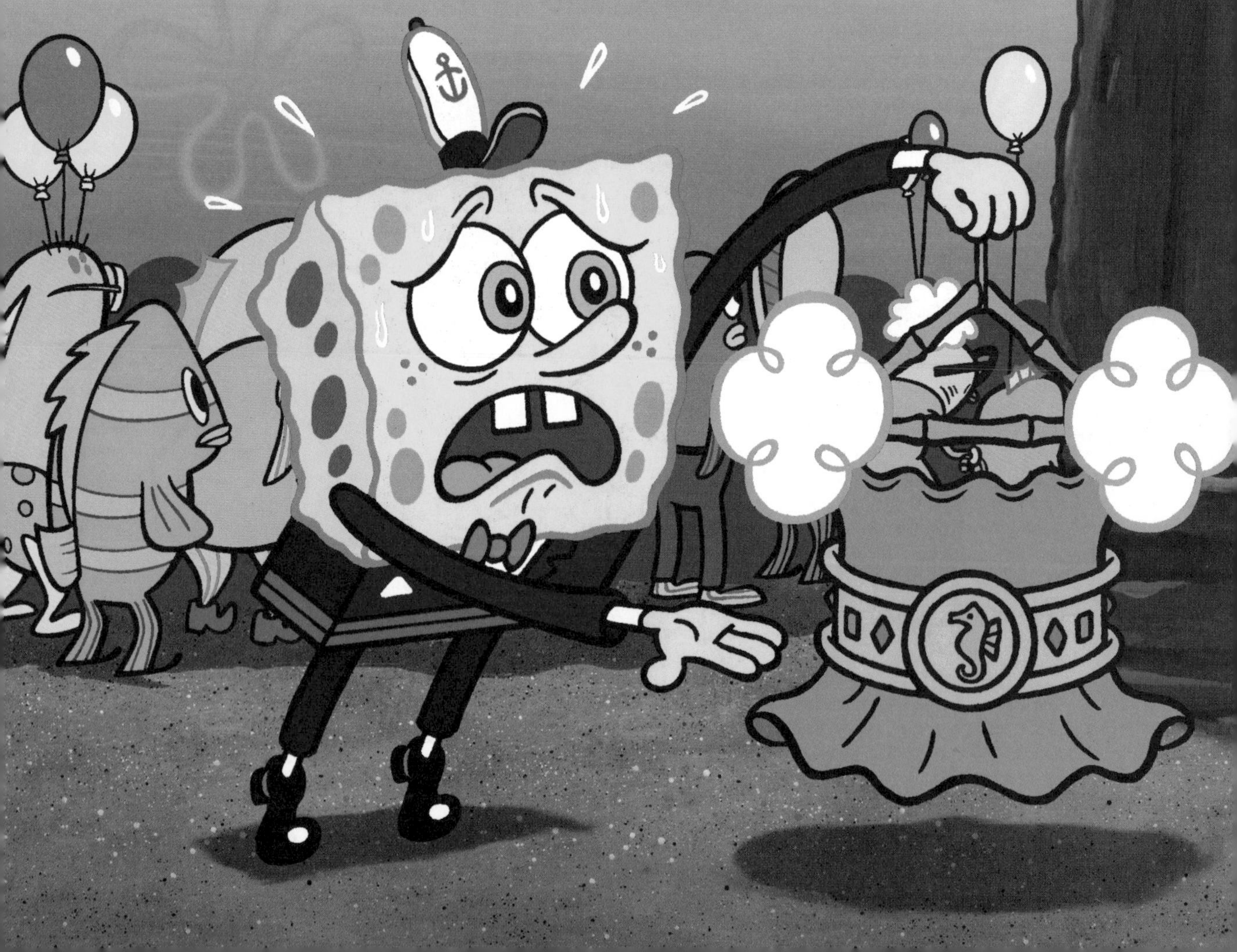

"No buts about it," said Patrick stubbornly. "I'm not going to look ridiculous in front of all those people." And he put on his beanie propeller hat and turned to walk away.

"But, Patrick," SpongeBob begged, "who am I going to get to be the princess?"

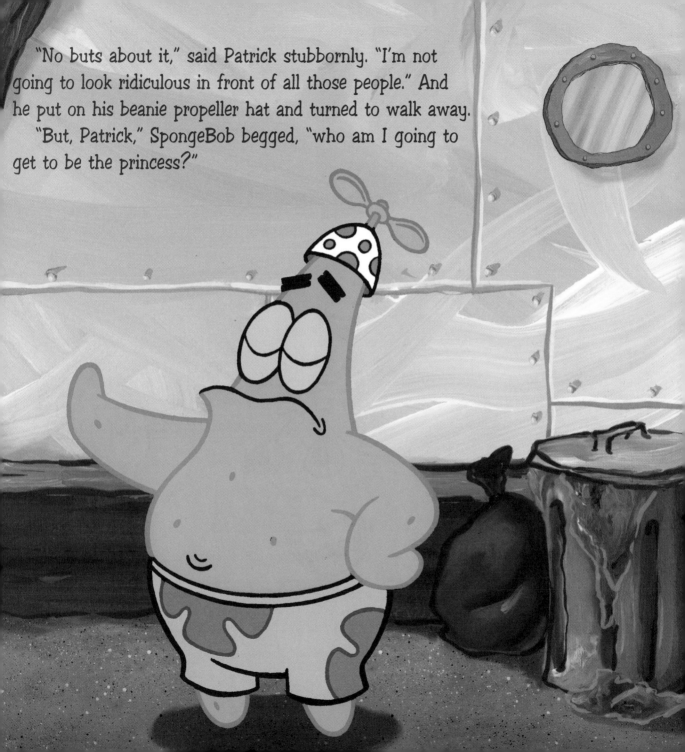

"Hello, loyal subjects from Bikini Bottom!" SpongeBob called to the crowd. "I am your princess!"

Everyone turned and stared at SpongeBob. "That's Princess Neptuna?" someone shouted.

"Of course I am!" squeaked SpongeBob. "Well, it's sure been great to see you. And now if you'll excuse me . . ."

"THAT'S NOT PRINCESS NEPTUNA!" said a guy with a very loud voice. "THAT'S JUST SOME GUY DRESSED UP IN A PRINCESS COSTUME!"

The crowd murmured angrily.

"GET HIM!" they yelled. Everyone started to rush toward SpongeBob!

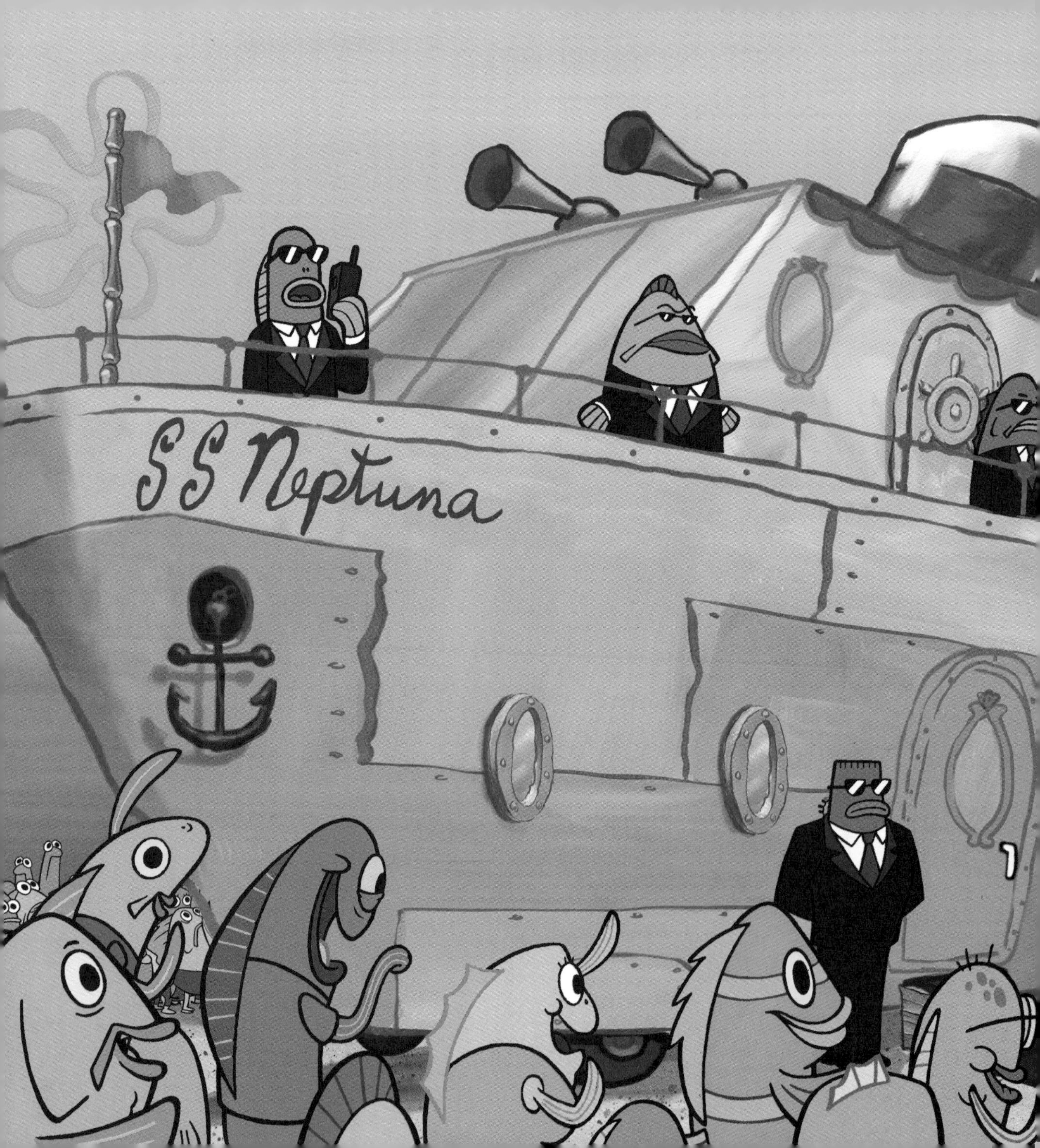
SS Neptuna

Before the crowd reached SpongeBob, a magnificent boat pulled up. The door opened, and a princess climbed out. "Hello, everyone," she said, smiling and waving. "I'm Princess Neptuna."

SpongeBob hoped he could remember the royalty lessons Squidward had given him. He bowed several times and got down on one knee. Taking her hand in his, SpongeBob said, "Hello, Princess Neptuna, what brings you to our humble establishment, the Krusty Krab?"

"Well," she answered, "I saw the crowd, so I stopped to see what was going on. I just *love* crowds!"

Princess Neptuna signed autographs for everyone—including Squidward. She even tried a Krabby Patty. "This Krabby Patty is a delicious morsel, SpongeBob," she said. "But it's a little messy."

SpongeBob brought over a box. "How would you like your very own box of Princess Napkins?" he asked.

The princess smiled. "You sure know how to treat a princess, SpongeBob!"